Spot Visits his Grandparents

Eric Hill

PUFFIN BOOKS

Hello, Grandma!
Hello, Grandpa!

Are you hungry already, Spot?

You can help me garden, Spot.

in the

I like helping you, Grandpa.

Do you want to eggs home?

take some

What have you found, Spot?

Whose ball is this, Grandpa?

Catch, Grandpa!

What have you been up to?

two

Time for a story before you go home, Spot.

Hello, Spot. How
with Grandma

was your day
and Grandpa?

It was great – and
look what
I found!

PUFFIN BOOKS

Published by the Penguin Group
Penguin Young Readers Group, 345 Hudson Street, New York, New York 10014, U.S.A.
Penguin Group (Canada), 10 Alcorn Avenue, Toronto, Ontario, Canada M4V 3B2
(a division of Pearson Penguin Canada Inc.)
Penguin Books Ltd, 80 Strand, London WC2R 0RL, England
Penguin Ireland, 25 St Stephen's Green, Dublin 2, Ireland
(a division of Penguin Books Ltd)
Penguin Group (Australia), 250 Camberwell Road, Camberwell,
Victoria 3124, Australia (a division of Pearson Australia Group Pty Ltd)
Penguin Books India Pvt Ltd, 11 Community Centre,
Panchsheel Park, New Delhi – 110 017, India
Penguin Group (NZ), Cnr Airborne and Rosedale Roads, Albany, Auckland 1310,
New Zealand (a division of Pearson New Zealand Ltd)
Penguin Books (South Africa) (Pty) Ltd, 24 Sturdee Avenue, Rosebank,
Johannesburg 2196, South Africa

Registered Offices: Penguin Books Ltd, 80 Strand, London WC2R 0RL, England

puffinbooks.com

First published by Frederick Warne & Co., 1995
Published in Puffin Books 1998
008-10 9 8

Copyright © Eric Hill, 1995
All rights reserved

The moral right of the author has been asserted

Printed and bound in Malaysia

ISBN-13: 978-0-14240-360-0